Foibles

By: **Allison McWood**

Annelid Press

Cover Design by: Daniel Greenhalgh

ISBN: 978-1-7771360-9-3

Cast List

FIFI SANDCASTLE ---An office clerk

NIGEL INKSPLOTCH ----------------------An office clerk/kleptomaniac

and compulsive liar

JOHN GRUNT------------------------An office clerk/sexist womanizer

BORIS PUTTERSON-- The boss

IDA DUNNIT --The secretary

ROBIN SLICK --- Fifi's ex-boyfriend

FONDA YOO --- Robin's girlfriend

GUS-- A security guard

MS. MUCHLY ---------------------------- executive assistant to the CEO

ACT ONE, SCENE ONE

> *The office of Ooford Inc. There is a bustle among the office clerks. IDA is seated at the front desk with a hands-free phone headset. Off to the side, BORIS is in the manager's office, leaning back in his swivel chair, his feet propped on his desk, talking on the phone at an unusual volume. Midstage, there are three desks. The first and third desks are occupied by NIGEL and GRUNT. The middle desk is still empty. IDA can be heard in the background, answering phones. She repeats, "Ooford Inc. One moment, please," over and over.*

BORIS   *(loudly, on phone)* I got numbers, Irv. Big numbers.

GRUNT   Nigel, have you seen my stapler?

NIGEL   *(stapling)* Check your desk drawer.

BORIS   *(on phone)* These numbers are huge, Irv. Lots and lots of big numbers.

> *Enter FIFI.*

IDA   Morning, Fifi.

FIFI   Morning, Ida.

BORIS   *(on phone)* I'd share these numbers with you, Irv, but I'm not sure you can handle their largeness.

> *FIFI removes her coat and sits at her desk.*

GRUNT   Wanna' neck?

FIFI   I'm ignoring you.

GRUNT   I saw how you swaggered those sizzling butt cheeks past my desk.

FIFI   I rebuke thee.

NIGEL   *(taking FIFI's lamp when she isn't looking, putting it on his desk)* Grunt, this is a place of business.

GRUNT   I'm talking to the uterus. Do you mind?

FIFI   Don't call me that...Where's my desk lamp?

BORIS   *(on phone)* My numbers are bigger than yours.

FIFI   Mr. Putterson talking to Irv about his numbers?

NIGEL   *(pocketing pen from FIFI's desk when her head is turned)* How did you know?

BORIS   Now if you'll excuse me, Irv, I am about to spin myself dizzy in my swivel chair.

NIGEL   Fifi, business.

FIFI   I get it, Nigel. What do you want to discuss?

NIGEL   The Maygrover Account.

FIFI   I'm on it, Nigel. I...*(phone rings)*...Excuse me...*(answers phone)* Fifi Sandcastle.

GRUNT   *(on phone at his desk)* Wanna' neck?

FIFI   *(on phone)* John Grunt, what have I told you about phoning me from your desk?

GRUNT   *(on phone)* You like it.

NIGEL   *(putting his finger on FIFI's dial)* Another personal call, Fifi?

FIFI   Grunt was just...

NIGEL   Didn't you tell him we're engaged?

FIFI   No.

NIGEL   Why?

FIFI   Because we aren't.

BORIS   *(loudly, on phone)* Bobby! My offspring! My loin

fruit! The first born of my five sperm dumplings! How are things with the product of my abnormally high testosterone levels?

FIFI   Nigel, why do you keep telling people we're engaged?

NIGEL   Because we are. You just don't know it yet. Now about the Maygrover Account...

FIFI   I've nearly closed the deal.

NIGEL   Have you, now?

FIFI   They bought the slogan. I'm just waiting on the CEO to return my call.

NIGEL   I gave you Maygrover.

FIFI   I am aware.

NIGEL   Because I love you.

FIFI   Go away.

NIGEL   Did I mention that I dated Molly Ringwald?

FIFI   Shut up. You did not.

NIGEL   I also had scantily clad models hanging all over me when I did business in Paris.

FIFI   How is that possible?

NIGEL   But you are special, Fifi. To you, I gave Maygrover.

FIFI   So you've mentioned.

NIGEL   You're my friend, Feef. I care about you.

FIFI   Remove yourself.

NIGEL   You need this account to prove yourself to Mr. Putterson.

BORIS   *(on phone)* Boris Putterson here. How the heck are ya?

FIFI   I've been working here longer than you have, Nigel.

NIGEL   Even so. You've heard about Mr. Putterson's plans.

FIFI   Plans?

NIGEL   You haven't heard.

FIFI   What plans?

NIGEL   *(without FIFI noticing, he takes money from her wallet)* My point being, I have job security. I don't have to prove myself the way you do.

FIFI   How have you proven yourself more so than I have?

NIGEL   Need I remind you of my pork slogan?

FIFI   Sweet Mary and Joseph. Not the pork slogan.

NIGEL   *Nothing says I love you like pork.*

FIFI   I can't believe they bought it.

NIGEL   Poetry.

FIFI   Slop.

NIGEL   *(without FIFI noticing, unplugs her computer monitor and carries it away)* That slogan won me corporate recognition. Unlike anything you've conjured, Little Lady.

FIFI   I've thought up dozens of...

NIGEL   Makes little difference what you've thought up. Mine's the slogan they bought.

FIFI   Subjective.

NIGEL   I want you to stick around. The Maygrover Account could be your only hope, given Mr. Putterson's plans.

FIFI   What plans?

NIGEL   It's a harsh world, Fifi. Someone's gotta' look out for you.

FIFI   I don't really need...

NIGEL   We're alike in many ways.

FIFI   God, help me.

NIGEL   We share the same roots.

FIFI   We went to the same freaking, junior high school.

NIGEL   Trust me.

FIFI   Trust y...Nigel, you are a compulsive liar. You lied to me about your age, your dating history, your   extra toe. You lied about your cat. You don't even have a cat. Who lies about a cat?

NIGEL   So, dinner tonight?

FIFI   What else are you lying about? Are you an international terrorist? A rhinoceros poacher? A woman? A kleptomaniac?

                           NIGEL's eyes widen.

FIFI   *(turning to use computer)* Nigel, I...*(noticing missing monitor)* Oh, dear God.

NIGEL   Maygrover. I gave you Maygrover.

FIFI   *(face down on her desk)* For which I am eternally in your debt.

NIGEL   *(taking FIFI's hat from the hat rack on his way out)* The account must not be botched.

FIFI   *(facedown)* Go ahead. Take the hat. I didn't like it anyway.

ACT ONE, SCENE TWO

BORIS's office. BORIS is lounging in his swivel chair.

BORIS   Foofoo!

Enter FIFI.

FIFI   Yes, Mr. Putterson?

BORIS   I have plans.

FIFI   So I've heard.

BORIS   What have you heard?

FIFI   That you have plans.

BORIS   That it?

FIFI   That's all I heard. Are these plans involving me?

BORIS   Sit down, Foofoo.

FIFI   I'd rather stand.

BORIS   It's best that you sit.

FIFI   But...

BORIS   You're all delicate like. You might get dizzy and swoon.

FIFI   I'll chance it.

BORIS   Foofoo...

NIGEL   *(popping his head in)* Her name is Fifi. Not Foofoo.

FIFI   Yes. You see, a name like Foofoo would be silly.

BORIS   *(bobbing his head and doing the finger-gun)* Nigel. How the heck are ya? Why don't you have yourself a raise?

NIGEL   Don't mind if I do. And Mr. Putterson?

BORIS   Boris.

NIGEL   Boris it is. Take extra care of my Fifi.

FIFI   Your?

NIGEL   We share roots.

                         Exit NIGEL.

FIFI   About the plans.

BORIS   I like him.

FIFI   Boris...

BORIS	The name's Mr. Putterson.
FIFI	Mr. Putterson, what are your plans?
BORIS	You're not sitting.
FIFI	*(sitting)* I'm sitting. Now can you...
BORIS	I like that Nigel. He's a nice lad.
FIFI	Does this have something to do with the Maygrover Account?
BORIS	I think I'll give Nigel a raise.
FIFI	You just did.
BORIS	He could use another. I'll write a memo to Ida.
FIFI	Mr. Putterson...
BORIS	Nigel deserves it. Do you recall his highly inspirational pork slogan?
FIFI	Not the pork slo...
BORIS	Nothing says I love you like pork. Don't those words move you?
FIFI	Like a wave of nausea.
BORIS	Makes me want to run out and buy some salted pork rind.

FIFI	That account had nothing to do with pork. He was selling throat lozenges.
BORIS	That's the genius of it.
FIFI	Mr. Putterson...
BORIS	Why can't you write slogans like that, Foofoo?
FIFI	I have a portfolio filled with slogans.
BORIS	Not about pork.
FIFI	That is the only slogan Nigel has written in the entire three years he's been working here.
BORIS	He doesn't need to write any more slogans. That pork slogan has one hundred times proven his worthiness. You, on the other hand, need to get your sizzling butt cheeks in gear.
FIFI	You've been talking to John Grunt.
BORIS	Such a nice lad.
FIFI	Mr. Putterson...
BORIS	Why are you here?
FIFI	You called me in to talk about your plans.
BORIS	Hold on a minute. I'm going to buzz Ida. *(buzzes)* You don't have a buzzer, do you, Foofoo? What am

I saying? Of course you don't.

Enter IDA.

IDA   You buzzed?

BORIS   Ida. Need a stack of new business cards made up. Pronto.

IDA   *(writing on a pad)* Got it. What would you like printed on them, Mr. Putterson?

BORIS   I'm going out on a limb here, but I'd say my name with my occupation printed directly below.

IDA   Occupation.

BORIS   That's what I said, Ida.

IDA   What exactly is it that you do?

BORIS   I...think of something.

IDA   Yes, Mr. Putterson.

Exit IDA.

FIFI   Mr. Putterson?

BORIS   Are you still here?

FIFI   Your plans?

BORIS   Plans. Yes. You're being outsourced.

FIFI   *(shocked, holding back emotion)* I...You're...Um... What?

BORIS   Outsourced.

FIFI   Um...why?

BORIS   No reason. I'm eventually going to outsource the entire department and I'm starting with you.

FIFI   Why me?

BORIS   You are inept.

FIFI   What?

BORIS   Inept. I learned that word this morning and I've been waiting all day to use it.

FIFI   What about Nigel Inksplotch and John Grunt?

BORIS   They'll be outsourced in their turn. Never you worry. My plan is to hold on to them as long as I can because they impress me.

FIFI   You're outsourcing the entire department.

BORIS   It really is a clever plan. With you gone, I'll have one less person to supervise. Less work for me. Catch my drift?

FIFI   Mr. Putterson...

BORIS   With each person I outsource, I'll have less and less work to do.

FIFI   Mr. Putterson...

BORIS   When I outsource my last employee, I'll have infinite time to bob my head and do the pretentious finger-gun thing.

FIFI   Mr. Putterson, if you please...

BORIS   What is it, Foofoo?

FIFI   If you outsource the entire department, you'll have no work left to do. Your job will be obsolete.

BORIS   Come again?

FIFI   You could be fired.

BORIS   But...I have this swivel chair.

FIFI   *(holding back tears)* I have been working here for five years. You're talking to me as though I'm unimportant.

BORIS   You are unimportant.

FIFI   Excuse me?

BORIS   Dispensable.

FIFI	*(trying to be strong)* What?
BORIS	*(smug)* Are you going to emote?
FIFI	Emote?
BORIS	Women emote.
FIFI	*(refusing to cry)* I refuse to emote.
BORIS	*(leaning back in his swivel chair, smirking with his feet on the desk)* Go ahead. Weep. I'm watching.
FIFI	I've been working at Ooford longer than you have.
BORIS	This isn't a competition.
FIFI	I didn't invest five years of my life to this company so I could...
BORIS	Foofoo, you know as well as I do that when you have a baby...
FIFI	Wait a minute. Baby?
BORIS	Let me finish.
FIFI	I am not having a baby.
BORIS	Women have babies. That's what they do. Meanwhile, we'll have to pay a temp, send you a mat leave cheque...

FIFI	I'm not even dating anyone.
BORIS	Hiring women is economically imprudent.
FIFI	I don't want a baby. Ever.
BORIS	That's not your decision to make.
FIFI	My job...
BORIS	There's no shame in it, Foofoo. Women have to be good at something.
FIFI	I am extremely good at what I do!
BORIS	*(smirking)* Riiiight.
FIFI	My job...
BORIS	If you need a job that badly, you can apply for Ida's job.
FIFI	What about Ida?
BORIS	Maternity leave.
FIFI	Ida is not having a baby.
BORIS	Give her time.
FIFI	I don't want to be a secretary.

BORIS   Women are good at jobs like that. And when your time comes, we can easily replace you.

FIFI   What about the Maygrover Account?

BORIS   Come again?

FIFI   The account I've been slaving over for the past six months?

BORIS   Finish it up and then you can clean out your desk.

FIFI   It's not that simple. This account is giving me leads to other opportunities. No one else will have the insight or the connections I have.

BORIS   *(smug)* You're squirming.

FIFI   If I can make this account work...

BORIS   *(smug)* You're going to cry.

FIFI   If I can make this account work...

BORIS   *(smug)* Squirm, squirm, squirm.

FIFI   My job means too much to me...Mr. Putterson, please...

ACT ONE, SCENE THREE

NIGEL and GRUNT are at their desks.

NIGEL   Fifi's coming out of Boris's office.

GRUNT   Fifi. *(howls)*

NIGEL   She's crying.

GRUNT   Women do that.

NIGEL   He did it again. Boris made Fifi cry. I can't believe Boris would make Fifi cry. I mean, look at her. How can you look at something that looks like that and make it cry?

GRUNT   Her emotions are feeble. It isn't difficult.

NIGEL   If anyone is going to make Fifi cry, it should be me.

GRUNT   Arooo!

NIGEL   Grunt, would you cut that out? Fifi is not yours to howl at.

GRUNT   She likes it.

NIGEL   Please.

GRUNT   Why else would she egg me on with all those

playful retorts of disgust?

NIGEL You can squelch all your carnal little thoughts. Fifi belongs to me.

GRUNT Since when?

NIGEL Since junior high school.

GRUNT So we'll both take her. Monogamy is overrated.

NIGEL Fifi has been infatuated with me ever since I sat next to her in Trig.

GRUNT Trig?

NIGEL It's math. You wouldn't have heard of it.

GRUNT Oh.

NIGEL She very coyly turned down all six of my invitations to the grad dance.

GRUNT The minx.

NIGEL And you see the way she looks at me with that desirous grimace.

GRUNT Horny wench.

NIGEL She's under my spell.

GRUNT   And yet, evident are the unchristian thoughts she has of my chiseled body. We both know that lust outranks infatuation.

NIGEL   Stay out of this, Grunt. Fifi is mine. I've invested a lot of time in taming her. I have control...

GRUNT   You have control over all women.

NIGEL   Control is complex. Women have peculiar minds. It takes years of intense, cerebral acrobatics to manipulate the female brain.

GRUNT   But...we're bigger than them.

NIGEL   Do you think this complex relationship Fifi and I have just happened overnight?

GRUNT   I can work my magic overnight.

NIGEL   She's mine.

GRUNT   Didn't anyone ever teach you to share?

NIGEL   She needs me, Grunt. Without me, Fifi is dizzy and confused like a lost...drunk...puppy.

GRUNT   So Fifi is being outsourced. Another one will come along. A foxy temp or a cleaning lady. Grab one of them. They're all the same.

NIGEL   Fifi needs me. She can't survive outside this building without me. What if she dies?

GRUNT   Nigel, you're not paying attention. You can have all the women you want. There isn't a woman in the world we can't take. We have complete contro...

Enter MS. MUCHLY, dressed in a skin tight shirt, very short skirt and extremely high heels. Seductively and powerfully, she walks across the stage, past NIGEL and GRUNT, who stare stupidly at her, mouths gaping defenselessly. MS. MUCHLY leans provocatively, toying with a piece of paper, supposedly an important document. NIGEL and GRUNT, helpless and stunned, turn their heads towards MS. MUCHLY, towards each other and then towards the audience.

GRUNT   Ms. Muchly.

NIGEL   The executive assistant to the CEO.

GRUNT   She scares the crap out of me.

NIGEL   Do you suppose she has a first name?

GRUNT   I'm not asking her. She might eat me for breakfast.

NIGEL   She must have a first name. After all, she's human, right?...Right?...Grunt, why are you not answering me?

GRUNT   I've been crippled with fear.

NIGEL   I thought...

GRUNT   ShutuphereshecomesIdon'twanttodiehere
             shecomesshutup.

                                    *MS.   MUCHLY   saunters
                                    powerfully   and   seductively
                                    towards NIGEL   and   GRUNT,
                                    who are stiff with terror. She
                                    menacingly leans in towards
                                    NIGEL   and   GRUNT,   who
                                    exaggeratedly lean back   in
                                    their chairs the closer she
                                    comes to their faces.*

NIGEL   We meant no harm, your worship. We were just
             wondering...I mean, it's none of our business,
             really...but we were wondering about your...first
             name?

MUCHLY   Mizzzzzzz.

GRUNT   *(mousy)* Please don't eat me.

                                    *MS. MUCHLY saunters away.
                                    NIGEL and GRUNT'S stunned
                                    and helpless stares follow MS.
                                    MUCHLY as she leaves.*

NIGEL   She doesn't have a first name. I told you she isn't human. She's a dragon...Grunt?

GRUNT   I can't feel my legs.

                              Enter BORIS, followed by FIFI
                              and IDA.

BORIS   Staff meeting, Gentlemen. Let's make this quick.
             I've got numbers to count.

NIGEL   Grunt, Ms. Muchly is gone. You can stop
             whimpering.

BORIS   Morale.

FIFI   Excuse me?

BORIS   Morale is the topic we'll be covering at today's
             meeting.

FIFI   We never have meetings.

BORIS   I am a leader. Just doing my job, Foofoo.

NIGEL   Fifi.

BORIS   Same thing.

FIFI   Mr. Putterson...

BORIS   I want everyone to think of ways we can boost
             morale in this office.

Everyone thinks.

BORIS   Now forget all those things.

FIFI   Forget about the ways we can boost morale?

BORIS   I disagree with morale.

IDA   *(writing memo)* Then what is the point of this meeting?

BORIS   The CEO claims that our department is below the acceptable point on the morale graph. I told him there is more than enough morale in my department and frankly, I agree with myself.

FIFI   Morale has never seen the inside of this room.

BORIS   What are you talking about? I bring in doughnuts every Friday.

FIFI   You don't share them with us.

BORIS   That does it. Foofoo is being insubordinate. This is precisely the reason why morale is dangero...

                              MS. MUCHLY crosses stage. NIGEL, GRUNT and BORIS stare at MS. MUCHLY with stunned, terrified looks on their faces.

FIFI   Please.

Exit FIFI and IDA.

MS. MUCHLY exits, followed by the terrified stares of the men.

After a brief pause, BORIS, NIGEL and GRUNT snap out of their trances.

BORIS   Morale is overrated.

GRUNT   You believe that?

BORIS   Very muchly. Er, Ms. Er...Where is Foofoo?

NIGEL   Fifi.

BORIS   I did not dismiss her. Can't tell a woman anything. And she wonders why she's being outsourced.

ACT ONE, SCENE FOUR

IDA's desk. IDA wearing a hands-free headset, occasionally answering calls.

FIFI   Outsourced. How can I compete with pork? If that insatiable boss of mine sets swine as his highest standard... I convinced Mr. Putterson to hold on to me long enough to prove myself with the Maygrover Account. But nothing I do impresses him. Nothing I do amounts to the marketing wizardry of his golden boy, Nigel Inksplotch. Ida, I'm good at what I do. I don't want to be plucked out by some insectivorous tyrant who makes me want to cry and then gets all smug about it. Arg! Mr. Putterson grinds at my last nerve! Hear me when I say this, Ida. I am not a frigging machine!

IDA   You need a baby.

FIFI   What?

IDA   I have four, little bundles who dropped straight from Heaven, yes they did. And look how gosh darned chipper I am.

FIFI   Fifi, what I need is...

IDA   A man.

FIFI   A what?

IDA	Can't have a baby without a man.
FIFI	I don't need this.
IDA	After all, you're thirty years old.
FIFI	Twenty-Nine.
IDA	Which doesn't leave us much time.
FIFI	Us?
IDA	We'll find you a man.
FIFI	When you say us.
IDA	Haven't you ever noticed how unusually gleeful I am?
FIFI	It's quite irritating, actually.
IDA	It's all because of my dear Samuel.
FIFI	Not the Samuel thing again.
IDA	Samuel and I are as cheery as two people can be. Atwitter like two, yellow parakeets on a branch.
FIFI	Too much information.
IDA	I just want to kiss him all over his cute, little puppy face.

FIFI	Awkward moment.
IDA	And our four, freckled angels. The day they cuddled their way into my life was the day I became alive.
FIFI	I'll be leaving now.
IDA	I'll find you a bloke who can make all this happen for you.
FIFI	I cared about someone once.
IDA	And?
FIFI	And I'm over him.
IDA	You're not over him.
FIFI	I am so over him.
IDA	If you were over him, you wouldn't say you were over him.
FIFI	I have never been more over a person in my life.
IDA	How many relationships have you been in?
FIFI	Counting the guy I'm over...One.
IDA	One.
FIFI	Shut up.

IDA   One jerk and now you're never going to trust another man ever again.

FIFI   He was not a je...

IDA   Give me twenty minutes. I'll find you an appropriate gentlemen caller.

FIFI   Ida...

IDA   I have someone in mind.

FIFI   No.

IDA   Imagine a mythological god with a game show host smile and an adorable, little...

FIFI   Ida...

IDA   Nose. I was going to say nose.

FIFI   What if this isn't what I want?

IDA   Are you caffeine deprived? What woman doesn't want babies?

FIFI   I want to explore possibilities with my career. My job excites me.

IDA   And mine excites me. When that phone rings, I have absolutely no idea who it will be on the line. What intrigue!

FIFI I want more than a foof job that does nothing more than put cheerios on the table. I want to suc...ceed. Ida, that didn't come out right. I'm sorry.

IDA Don't be. I have succeeded.

Enter BORIS.

BORIS Ida, what the heck is taking you so long with my new batch of business cards?

IDA Here they are. I even bound them with an elastic band.

BORIS *(reading business card)* Boris Putterson. Completely Incompetent...I like it.

Exit BORIS.

FIFI Very nice.

IDA I'm quite the wit, yes. Now about your man...

FIFI No blind dates, Ida. Nothing good can come of them.

IDA I'm ignoring you.

FIFI Ida, why must you...

IDA I'm meddlesome.

ACT ONE, SCENE FIVE

NIGEL and GRUNT's desks. BORIS is off to the side, in his office, talking on the phone.

BORIS   *(on phone)* The name's Boris Putterson. Completely Incompetent.

NIGEL   Forget about Ms. Muchly.

GRUNT   How did she become so powerful?

BORIS   *(on phone)* Numbers.

NIGEL   We have the power. Remember?

FIFI walks by.

GRUNT   Oh. Yesssss.

BORIS   Speaking of numbers, I have five, count 'em, five kids. Although that has nothing to do with our business relationship, I thought it might give you some indication as to how virile I am.

Buzz.

NIGEL   *(answering phone)* What is it, Ida?

IDA   *(on hands-free phone from her desk)* Your new client's here, Mr. Inksplotch.

NIGEL   *(on phone)* Send him in. *(hangs up)* New client. Something to do with hair products.

GRUNT   Hair products?

NIGEL   Challenging, I know. But I have developed a reputation for myself. Pork.

GRUNT   Pork. Lucky bastar...*(notices ROBIN entering)* What's with Vidal Sassoon?

ROBIN   Nigel Inksplotch?

NIGEL   Last time I checked.

ROBIN   Robin Slick. I'm in hair products.

GRUNT   No kidding.

NIGEL   Have a seat, Mr. Slick. I'll just...

ROBIN   *(noticing FIFI)* Clarissa?

NIGEL   What? No, that's Fifi.

ROBIN   Clarissa Sandcastle.

NIGEL   Her name is Fifi. And you can stop looking at her because she belongs to...

FIFI   Robin?

NIGEL   You know each other. Terrific. Now about the hair products...

FIFI   I think I have to leave.

ROBIN   Clarissa,   wait!...Hold   on   a   minute,   Mr.
              Inksplotch...Clarissa...

FIFI   Robin...

ROBIN   It's been a long time.

FIFI   Robin...

ROBIN   Why does everyone keep calling you Fifi?

NIGEL   Because that's her name.

ROBIN   Her given name?

NIGEL   I gave it to her.

ROBIN   Fifi?

NIGEL   She reminds me of a French maid. The name sort of
              stuck.

GRUNT   You mean her name's not really Fifi?

BORIS   *(on phone)* Let's talk numbers.

ROBIN   Clarissa, maybe we should...

FIFI	This isn't the time, Robin.
NIGEL	Yes, this isn't the time, Robin. We were about to discuss mousse.
FIFI	I have this Maygrover Account.
BORIS	*(loudly, on phone)* I thought you, along with everyone else in the room, would like to hear about my numbers.
ROBIN	I have to see you, Clarissa. It's important. Are you busy tonight?
NIGEL	You heard the woman. She's working on the Maygrover Account. She'll be working late.
FIFI	I'll be working late.
ROBIN	Afterwards?
FIFI	I have a date.
NIGEL	A wha? With who? A guy? Who is he?
FIFI	Nigel, stop. It's no big deal.
NIGEL	You didn't tell me anything about this this this, what did you call it? A date?
FIFI	A blind date. Ida set me up.
NIGEL	Damn that Ida.

ROBIN	I'll be waiting at La Maison Cochon.
FIFI	La Maison Cochon? That's where we...
ROBIN	If the blind date doesn't work out...
FIFI	I'll...I'll think about it.
ROBIN	*(kissing FIFI's hand)* I'll be waiting.
FIFI	*(momentarily entranced)* You...you have such nice hair.
ROBIN	I know, Love. I know.

> *ROBIN attempts to leave.*

NIGEL	Wait a minute! We have not yet discussed mousse or products of the mousse persuasion!
ROBIN	Tomorrow, Mr. Inksplotch. Today, I have much on my mind.

> *ROBIN blows FIFI a kiss. Exit ROBIN.*

FIFI	*(smitten whimper)*
NIGEL	So who's the guy with the hair?
FIFI	I'm not obligated to share my personal life with...

NIGEL	Personal? How personal?
FIFI	Nigel...
NIGEL	You've never kept anything from me before. We've had conjoined souls since the sixth grade.
FIFI	No we haven't.
NIGEL	Come on, Feef. You've always told me everything.
FIFI	Only because you harp on me until I squeeze out every minute detail of my life.
NIGEL	That hurts, Fifi. It really does.
FIFI	Stay out of it.
GRUNT	You have to admit, the guy does have great hair.
FIFI	He came back. This must mean...
NIGEL	What does this mean, Fifi?
FIFI	This must mean...
NIGEL	Why does he keep calling you Clarissa?
FIFI	He came back.
NIGEL	Fifi, what's happening to us?

ACT ONE, SCENE SIX

FIFI's desk, after hours. She is alone, working at something that is creating a fair bit of paper and exhaustion. She is rather askew.

FIFI
Maygrover. Maygrover. *(yawns)* Maygr...*(checks watch)* For Pete's sake. *(picks up phone)* Security? I need an escort to my car. *(hangs up)* Stupid, blind date. I'll never get home in time now.

Enter GUS, in security guard uniform.

GUS
Evening, Clarissa. Need some company to your car? Parking lot's quite dark tonight.

FIFI
Thanks, Gus. I'll be a minute. Do you have time to wait here a sec?

GUS
Take your time.

FIFI
This day.

GUS
Tough one? *(unwraps a chocolate bar)*

FIFI
Were you aware that Mr. Putterson is planning on outsourcing this entire department?

GUS
From what you've told me about him, it sounds typical.

FIFI   Starting with me! He would have sent me packing this morning, but I convinced him to keep me on long enough to prove myself with the Maygrover Account.

GUS   Good for you.

FIFI   But these hours. I haven't eaten since breakfast.

                                GUS offers his chocolate bar to FIFI, who takes it and eats.

FIFI   It doesn't help that I'm sandwiched between the perv and the raving lunatic. Grunt is forever making crude passes at me and Nigel...

GUS   Does he still steal stuff from your desk?

FIFI   My hole punch. My computer monitor. My wallet.

GUS   *(handing wallet to FIFI)* Does he still tell lies?

FIFI   About everything. How much money he makes. His middle name. His rare disease. But the lie that irks me the most...

GUS   He goes around telling everyone you've been infatuated with him since the sixth grade.

FIFI   Exactly. And there's nobody I could be less attracted to, Gus. Not only is he a compulsive lying kleptomaniac, he's funny-looking and he smells like boiled broccoli.

GUS   *(handing Clarissa the hat which NIGEL stole earlier)*
                       Oh, Clarissa.

FIFI   Nigel irritates me like a chafing rash. And he started
                       this Fifi thing. Everyone in this god-forsaken
                       building keeps calling me Fifi because of Nigel and
                       his French maid fetish.

GUS   That must make you feel...

FIFI   I just go with it. Nobody listens to me anyway.

GUS   You mentioned the Maygrover Account.

FIFI   I have to do great things with this assignment.

GUS   You will.

FIFI   You don't understand, Gus. Mr. Putterson is
                       waiting for me to mess up.

GUS   Did he try to make you cry again, while smirking
                       smugly in his swivel chair?

FIFI   He did.

GUS   The jerk.

FIFI   Nobody cares, Gus.

GUS   Can I take that stack of papers for you?

                                       FIFI plops the stack of papers

into GUS's arms.

FIFI   Something happened to me today. Something unusual.

GUS   Hmmm?

FIFI   My ex showed up.

GUS   Robin?

FIFI   The very one.

GUS   Oh my.

FIFI   Would you believe he's Nigel's new client? He's in hair products now.

GUS   Sounds appropriate.

FIFI   It's weird, Gus. Seeing him again after...

GUS   You don't need to say it. I can understand how you must feel.

FIFI   If you understand, then explain it to me.

GUS   Sorry?

FIFI   I'm not sure how I feel.

GUS   But he...

FIFI

I know. But no man is perfect. You have to accept the bad with the good. Like a package.

GUS

You mean you're considering...

FIFI

I don't know what I'm considering. I tried to blow him off, but he asked me to meet him at La Maison Cochon.

GUS

Isn't that the restaurant where...

FIFI

Yes.

GUS

Oh my.

FIFI

If I didn't have this stupid, blind date tonight...

GUS

Poor thing.

FIFI

What do I do?

GUS

You need to figure out how you feel.

FIFI

It's too hard! I mean, Robin...He's...Come on, Fifi. You're not eighteen anymore.

GUS

Your name is Clarissa.

FIFI

I can't stop thinking about him.

GUS

Robin.

FIFI   It took me years to get over him. I thought I had.

GUS   Have you?

FIFI   Gus, I never threw out his phone number. Why do you suppose that is?

GUS   You're a masochist?

FIFI   You're right. How can I trust him after...I mean, I never trusted another man for years after he...Men can't be trusted.

GUS   Sometimes they can.

FIFI   Never. Men are creeps.

GUS   Well, I...

FIFI   But Robin could have changed. It's been several years. After all, he finally quit that hypnotist gig got a respectable career in hair products.

GUS   Okay.

FIFI   But I have this blind date.

GUS   That you do.

FIFI   What have I gotten myself into?

GUS   What?

FIFI

Men are slime. I'm setting myself up for more disappointment.

GUS

Not ALL men...

FIFI

Come on, Gus. What do you know about men?

GUS

Well, I...

FIFI

On the other hand...

GUS

There's another hand?

FIFI

This could be the guy.

GUS

He could?

FIFI

Ida's pick. Who would have thought?

GUS

I thought...

FIFI

He could be just what I need to get my mind off Robin.

GUS

I suppose...

FIFI

I don't want to be alone forever.

GUS

You don't?

FIFI

I need to be independent. But independence can be lonely.

GUS   Sure can.

FIFI   And even if this blind date is keeping me from the man I'm destined to be with, it makes no difference because I'll probably never get married anyway.

GUS   Really.

FIFI   Marriage is an ideal. I can't have everything.

GUS   Oh.

FIFI   What I do need is a distraction.

GUS   A...

FIFI   Men are distractions. That's it. Distractions. I can just go out and have a good time and leave it at that.

GUS   What about...

FIFI   I am emotionally ill equipped to attach myself to a man. Men are so flippant.

GUS   Clarissa, I think...

FIFI   There's no time to think. I'm late.

                              GUS opens door for FIFI.

FIFI   Take me to my car.

ACT ONE, SCENE SEVEN

FIFI's apartment. GRUNT has let himself in and made himself comfortable on the couch. FIFI is not yet home. GRUNT snoops through some of FIFI's things and chortles mockingly at each item he finds. He stops abruptly when FIFI enters.

FIFI   *(gasps)* Grunt!

GRUNT   Wanna' neck?

FIFI   What in the world...

GRUNT   I took the liberty of having a key made.

FIFI   I'm not even going to try making sense of that. Just make yourself scarce. I have a blind date who should be arriving any time n...

GRUNT   I am he.

FIFI   You?

GRUNT   The blind date in question.

FIFI   I am going to rip off Ida's arm and hit her on the head with it.

GRUNT   Come on, Uterus. You know you want me.

FIFI   I want you to leave.

GRUNT   You can't mean that. I brought Cornish game hens.

FIFI   Cornish game hens?

GRUNT   I feel like something French. Drizzle something French on these, will you?

FIFI   Me?

GRUNT   Perhaps a nice rosemary jus.

FIFI   Grunt...

GRUNT   Do you speak French?

FIFI   What the...

GRUNT   I speak French. Would you like me to teach you?

FIFI   No.

GRUNT   Of course you do, Fifi. Or as they say in France, Fayfay.

FIFI   My name is not...

GRUNT   *(tossing hens at FIFI)* I'm starving. Or as they say in France, starvingay.

FIFI   That's not even French.

GRUNT   Oh, I think it is.

FIFI   Grunt...

GRUNT   Nigel tells me you remind him of a French maid.

FIFI   Of all the...out!

GRUNT   Is this how you treat all your dates? No wonder you're not married.

FIFI   Get out and take your jaundiced chickens with you.

GRUNT   Game hens.

FIFI   This whole evening was a mistake. I don't want you here. Do you understand?

GRUNT   Let's copulate.

FIFI   Not only is that morally repugnant, I don't even know you.

GRUNT   You're not giving me a chance. How is that fair?

FIFI   For the love of...Okay. Let's sit on this couch at a comfortable distance and get to know each other, if we absolutely must...That's not a comfortable distance, Grunt.

GRUNT   I'm comfortable with it.

FIFI   Grunt, that is inappropriate.

GRUNT   Prude.

FIFI   Shut up and talk.

GRUNT   Let's copulate.

FIFI   I'll talk first...So tell me, Grunt. What's on your mind? Don't answer that.

GRUNT   You remind me of my third wife.

FIFI   You never told me you were married. How many times?

GRUNT   I don't know. Four or five.

FIFI   What were their names?

GRUNT   I don't remember.

FIFI   The names of the women you were married to?

GRUNT   I think the second one began with the letter R.

FIFI   R! Lovely letter, the letter R.

GRUNT   Communication is overrated. Why don't we go in the other room and break the seventh commandment?

FIFI   Enough! Grunt, let's not do anything that will make things awkward at the office.

GRUNT   I lack morals. I'll be fine with it.

FIFI   Grunt, I don't want to...

GRUNT   You don't have a choice, woman. GRUNT grabs FIFI.

FIFI   I...

GRUNT   Come on, Fifi the French Maid. Or as they say in France, Fayfay the...

FIFI   Grunt!

GRUNT   I'm bigger than you.

> GRUNT aggressively attempts to kiss FIFI on the mouth, but FIFI turns her face and grimaces as he kisses the side of her cheek.

FIFI   (grimacing) I'm not consenting.

GRUNT   How can you say that after you led me on so?

FIFI   I never...

GRUNT   Wiggling around the office in those provocative, pinstriped suits. You're just asking for it.

FIFI   Provocative?

GRUNT   Those pants. They they they fit.

FIFI   Of course they fit.

GRUNT   You have no business wearing clothes that look nice on you. You're sending hormone-inducing messages.

FIFI   I can't look professional at work?

GRUNT   It's not fair to the perverts. We have rights too!

FIFI   What the...

GRUNT   You're making temptation nearly impossible to resist!

FIFI   Grunt...

GRUNT   If you don't want to be grabbed, pinched, assaulted, inappropriately touched or deflowered onsite, wear something frumpy. Something baggy and shapeless. Like burlap.

FIFI   I am a professional!

GRUNT   So are prostitutes. Or as they say in France, prositutay.

FIFI   (pushing GRUNT out the door) No one in France says anything of the kind. Get out before I call security.

GRUNT   As they say in France...

> *FIFI slams the door in GRUNT's face. After a moment of fuming, FIFI opens the door and throws the game hens at GRUNT. She closes the door behind her and cries.*

FIFI   Robin.

> *FIFI goes to her closet and takes out a box. She madly rummages through it.*

FIFI   I know I kept his number. I never threw anything out. *(finds ROBIN's picture)* Oh, Robin. You have such terrific hair. *(sets picture on table facing her. She waves at it and continues rummaging)* This night does not have to be entirely hellish. If I can only find Robin's cell number. I mean, he wouldn't have invited me to La Maison Cochon if he didn't want to...that's our restaurant. *(finds something)* A Christmas card. *(reads)* Clarissa, thanks for the red scarf. *(choked up)* Red scarf. I gave him a red scarf for Christmas and he thanked me for it. What a terrific guy. *(rummaging)* I have to find...find...find...*(finds something)* Robin's styling gel. I'm having a moment. *(looking at ROBIN's picture)* Oh, Robin. Nobody's perfect. Whatever went wrong who cares? I'm not petty. The important thing is how you make me feel. You make me feel eighteen again. *(rummaging)* The best thing about Robin is that he is nothing like Grunt or Nigel. He's charming. He's suave. He's well-coiffed. He's...*(finds something)* He better have his cell turned on.

> *FIFI scrambles to her phone and dials.*

FIFI *(on phone)* Robin? It's Clarissa. Are you still at La Maison Cochon? *(bites her fist in excitement)* That's lovely. Listen, my evening seems to be freed up so...You would? *(silently and vigorously bounces up and down with her face screwed up in excitement)* I suppose that will be fine...Excuse me? I'm your what?...You haven't called me that since...I am likewise looking forward to your company. I'll be arriving presently. *(hangs up)* Presently? *(hitting herself on the head)* Stupid!

ACT ONE, SCENE EIGHT

A table at La Maison Cochon. ROBIN is seated next to FONDA, who looks abruptly stunned all the time. FONDA is wearing a red scarf. Enter FIFI. ROBIN notices her and gets up to meet her at the entrance of the restaurant.

ROBIN   You made it.

FIFI   I made it.

ROBIN   Remember our table, Clarissa?

ROBIN leads FIFI by the hand to the table where FONDA is sitting. FONDA is wide-eyed as usual and looking around herself perpetually, somewhat like a stunned ostrich.

FONDA   *(looking around, confused)* Robin? Robin? Robin?

ROBIN   *(kisses FONDA)* I'm here, Love.

FIFI   Um, Robin...

ROBIN   *(sitting down)* Clarissa, I would like you to meet my girlfriend, Fonda.

FONDA	*(to FIFI)* I'm Fonda Yoo.

FIFI	How lovely. I wish the feeling was mutual.

FONDA	Was that a joke? Am I to laugh?

ROBIN	Yes, Fonda. That was a joke.

FONDA	*(laughing)* Oh, Clarissa! Robin never told me you were so witty!

FIFI	Robin fails to mention many things.

FONDA	Am I to laugh?

ROBIN	Go ahead and laugh...Clarissa, what are you doing?

FIFI	I'm not sure I know what you mean, Mr. Slick.

FONDA	I ordered squid for everyone.

ROBIN	*(patiently)* Fonda, I explained to you that it is impolite to...I'm sorry, Clarissa. I do hope you like squid.

FIFI	I liked a squid once.

ROBIN exhales.

FONDA	Robin? Did I do something wrong?

ROBIN	*(patiently)* I forgive you Fonda.

FIFI	So, Fonda. How do you feel about Robin having dinner with another woman?
ROBIN	*(warningly)* Clarissa...
FONDA	At first I was morose. Is that a good word, Robin? Morose?
ROBIN	Splendid word, Fonda.
FONDA	Many thank yous, Robin...At first, I was morose. But I soon forgave Robin because Robin is a charming fellow. I am fond of Robin.
FIFI	And I am sure that Robin is fonda' you too.
FONDA	But Robin is not Fonda Yoo. I am Fonda Yoo. I am confused in my head. Robin, you did not tell me that we have the same name.
ROBIN	*(patiently)* Fonda, what Clarissa just used is called a pun.
FONDA	Pun.
ROBIN	There's my clever girl.
FONDA	So you are still Robin?
ROBIN	Yes, Love.
FONDA	And I am still Fonda? Fonda Yoo?

ROBIN   That's right, Love.

FIFI   *(noticing FONDA's scarf)* What is that?

FONDA   I think it is a scarf. Hold on one minute while I check. Robin, is this a scarf?

ROBIN   Yes, Fonda. That is a scarf. A red scarf.

FONDA   Robin says this is a scarf. A red scarf.

FIFI   Where did it come from?

FONDA   A red sheep.

ROBIN   *(patiently)* Fonda, remember our little chat about speaking out loud?

FONDA   Forgive me, Robin. I was confused in my head.

ROBIN   I know, Love. I know.

FONDA   Do I still get to be your girlfriend?

ROBIN   Of course, Love.

FIFI   Robin, why is Fonda wearing that scarf?

ROBIN   Fonda looks stunning in red.

FIFI   You don't even remember when I gave it to you.

ROBIN   What?

FIFI   I gave you that scarf...

FONDA   Red scarf.

FIFI   That red scarf for Christmas.

ROBIN   That must have been something like eleven years ago.

FIFI   Even so...

ROBIN   What is the matter with you?

FIFI   Nothing is wrong with me, Mr. Slick. But I'm curious as to what transformed your personality since last we met.

ROBIN   Since last we met? Clarissa, I was in your office making a mousse transaction.

FONDA   Excuse me. Robin, I have to pee. What am I to do?

ROBIN   Go ahead and pee.

FONDA   Right here in front of everyone?

ROBIN   The ladies' room, Fonda.

FONDA   Without Robin?

ROBIN	*(putting leash on FONDA)* Excuse me, Clarissa. This will only take a minute.
	ROBIN leads FONDA away with a leash. FIFI does a double-take as they leave, then faces the audience with a stunned, yet disgusted look on her face. ROBIN re-enters.
ROBIN	She'll be a while. Toilets confuse her.
FIFI	I have to leave.
ROBIN	Don't be ridiculous. Sit.
FIFI	You expect me to stay?
ROBIN	We haven't seen each other in years. Now you're acting all weird. I think you owe me an...
FIFI	An explanation? You cocky little...It's a good thing you've got great hair.
ROBIN	What in the world has gotten into you?
FIFI	You're doing it again! The same thing you did to me eleven years ago!
ROBIN	What did I do?
FIFI	You strung me along, while secretly dating a flaky side of fries.

ROBIN   Secretly?

FIFI   Do you have a problem with brains? Does my intellect repulse you? What is this sick obsession you have with daft hussies?

ROBIN   Fonda!...Hold on.

                                FIFI waits impatiently for ROBIN to return with FONDA on the leash.

FIFI   Why didn't you tell me about Fonda?

ROBIN   I didn't think it mattered.

FIFI   You didn't think it...Robin, if you had no intentions of wooing me, then your behaviour in my office was completely inappropriate.

ROBIN   How so?

FIFI   You seduced me with your...with your hair and your blowing of kisses. You invited me to our restaurant.

ROBIN   Clarissa...

FIFI   Then on the phone you called me...*(embarrassed)* You called me your little espresso bean.

FONDA   Espresso bean? That is the name Robin called me once. Don't worry though. I explained to Robin that my name if Fonda. Fonda Yoo.

FIFI   Slut.

ROBIN   Fonda is not a...

FIFI   I was talking to you.

ROBIN   I call everyone my little espresso bean. Even my cousins.

FIFI   So all those times when we were dating...

FONDA   I hunger.

> *ROBIN takes out a dog dish, fills it with food and puts it on the floor. FONDA eats from the dish like a dog.*

ROBIN   Why are you belittling Fonda?

FIFI   You could have prepared me.

ROBIN   For what? We haven't dated in eleven years. Why did you think I invited you here?

FIFI   Insensitive son of a...

ROBIN   I'm charming. Is it my fault you took that the wrong way?

FIFI   *(leaving)* I remember now why I...why I...I don't need you.

ACT TWO, SCENE ONE

> *IDA's desk. BORIS brisk walks past the desk.*

IDA   Mr. Putterson?

BORIS   Need to be somewhere.

> *BORIS walks briskly past IDA's desk in the other direction.*

IDA   Where are you going?

BORIS   Somewhere important.

> *BORIS walks briskly past IDA's desk.*

IDA   Where exactly are you…

BORIS   I've somewhere important to be. Hence the brisk pace.

IDA   But Mr. Putterson…

> *BORIS's cell phone rings. BORIS speaks louder as though he is expecting everyone around him to be listening.*

BORIS	I am about to answer my cell phone! *(answers cell)* Irv! How the heck are ya!
IDA	Mr. Putterson?
BORIS	*(louder on cell)* I've got numbers, Irv. *(walks away)* Talk to me as I walk at a brisk pace to that very important spot on the other side of the building.

Exit BORIS. Enter FIFI.

IDA	How was your...
FIFI	Shut up.
IDA	Spill.
FIFI	No.
IDA	Didn't you have a good time with...
FIFI	You set me up with John Grunt.
IDA	Affectionate, little devil, isn't he?
FIFI	He strummed my bra strap like a ukulele.
IDA	Grunt said it went well.
FIFI	He would.
IDA	It didn't go well?

FIFI   I don't want to talk about it.

IDA   Fine. I'll find out one way or another what happened on your date. The walls are thin and Grunt has a big mouth.

Enter NIGEL.

NIGEL   Morning, Ida. Any messages?

IDA   The throat lozenge people called to see if you have any more pork slogans, your squash game is cancelled Friday, Fifi's date was a disaster and it's your turn to make the coffee.

NIGEL   *(perky)* Fifi's date was a disaster? What happened?

IDA   She won't tell me.

Enter GRUNT.

GRUNT   Morning.

NIGEL   Fifi's date was a disaster.

GRUNT   I was there.

Exit GRUNT.

NIGEL   You went on a date with Grunt?

FIFI   Robin.

NIGEL   Slick?

IDA   How many dates did you go on last night?

FIFI   What does it matter? Men are all the same.

NIGEL   So things didn't work out with you and Grackle?

FIFI   His name is Robin. Not Grackle.

NIGEL   If we're going steady, you need to tell me about things like this.

FIFI   Going steady? Nigel, we're not in junior high school.

NIGEL   There is an element of trust in any serious relationship.

FIFI   We do not have a...Ida, stop smiling...Nigel, we do not have a serious relationship.

NIGEL   I do cherish this cat and mouse thing we have. It's what makes our relationship what it is.

FIFI   Stop calling it a relationsh...Ida, what on earth are you smiling about?

IDA   I'm about to burst!

FIFI   You're always about to burst.

NIGEL   *(handing FIFI a small box)* Here.

FIFI   Nigel, what on earth?

IDA   Am I glowing?

NIGEL   Open it.

FIFI   *(opening box)* For Pete's sake. I...

NIGEL   You like?

IDA   Will someone please ask me why I'm glowing?

FIFI   I can't take this, Nigel.

NIGEL   It's a diamond necklace.

FIFI   I can see what it is.

IDA   Let's play a game. Guess how many people there are in this room...right now.

NIGEL   I'm losing you. I don't want to lose you, Fifi.

FIFI   Where on earth did you get the money to pay for this?

IDA   Hello?

FIFI   You can't just give me diamonds and expect me to...

IDA   Speaking of expecting...

NIGEL   My motives are pure. If you want to think of it as nothing more than a gesture of friendship, that's okay.

FIFI   If I do put it on, you must remember that this does not in any way, mean that you and I...

IDA   *(impatiently putting necklace on FIFI)* Just put on the freaking necklace and congratulate me!

FIFI   Ida, are you...

IDA   Number five!

> *BORIS brisk walks past IDA's desk, dropping something in front of IDA on his way by.*

BORIS   Walking briskly. Important man walking briskly. Walking. Walking.

IDA   Mr. Putterson, what's this?

BORIS   Your pink slip.

> *FIFI and NIGEL shy away, not wanting anything to do with the conversation.*

IDA   My what?

BORIS   Have your belongings packed in a box by the end of the day.

IDA   What for?

BORIS   You're having a baby.

IDA   And?

BORIS   You've abused your privilege to bear fruit.

IDA   There didn't seem to be a problem the last time I...

BORIS   Company policy dictates that there be a maximum of four children per employee. Any more than that is a blatant lack of self-control.

IDA   But...

BORIS   You've reached your limit. Tah.

IDA   Mr. Putterson, you have five children.

BORIS   That's different.

IDA   How so?

BORIS   I'm virile.

IDA   This is wrongful dismissal.

BORIS   Not according to company policy.

IDA   I've never heard of such a thing.

BORIS   How many maternity cheques do you expect us to scarf up, you little tart?

IDA   You're enjoying this.

BORIS   Yes.

IDA   Why?

BORIS   I have an aversion to women.

IDA   Mr. Putterson...

BORIS   What are you complaining about? You love being a mother. That's all you ever talk about.

IDA   Yes.

BORIS   So stay home and do it full time. What's the problem?

IDA   I'm not just a mother. I'm a woman too! In fact, I was a woman before I became a mother.

BORIS   Come again?

IDA   I like my job. It gives me dimension.

BORIS   If your job means so much to you, you should have practiced restraint!

IDA   You are completely incompetent!

BORIS   And don't you forget it!

ACT TWO, SCENE TWO

> *Coffee truck. FIFI is purchasing a coffee. MS. MUCHLY saunters over, pushing her way in front of FIFI.*

FIFI   Nice.

> *MS. MUCHLY gives FIFI an icy stare.*

FIFI   Bad enough I get kicked around by a bunch of emotionally dead men, now I have the freaking dragon lady pushing her way in front of me at the coffee truck.

MUCHLY   What did you just say?

FIFI   What makes you so much better than everyone else? Why do men recoil in terror at the very sight of you? Why do all the sexist double standards not apply to you?

MUCHLY   I am the executive assistant to the CEO.

FIFI   You're a secretary. Get over yourself.

MUCHLY   I am the most powerful woman in the entire company.

FIFI   And I'm getting outsourced after five years of dedication. Tell me, Ms. Muchly, where might a woman reach such a pinnacle of power?

MUCHLY   The answer is obvious, little girl.

FIFI   Obvious, hmm? Then why is Ida being fired for fulfilling her wifely duties and why is a seven-year-old on the other side of the ocean going to be doing my job at the end of the week?

MUCHLY   I can't believe you haven't figured it out.

FIFI   Figured what out? The world of business is saturated in testosterone. Why are you smirking?

MUCHLY   Women are the ones pressing the buttons. Women are the ones with the power. *(manipulating her lips around the word)* Wom-en.

FIFI   But men...

MUCHLY   Men just think they're in control. That's what we want them to believe.

FIFI   What the...

MUCHLY   We have what they want. We know about their Achilles heel.

FIFI   But we don't have equal rights.

MUCHLY   No. We have more rights.

FIFI   What the...

MUCHLY   How do you think I achieved so much power? Hazard a guess.

FIFI   I couldn't even...

MUCHLY   I used to be an envelope-licker until one day, Howard from Payroll brushed up against me in the elevator. I reported him to HR for touching me inappropriately. Howard was fired and I got bumped up to the seventeenth floor.

FIFI   But...

MUCHLY   Then I put drywall dust on my hands and grabbed my own butt. You wouldn't believe how many chumps I got fired before I made it to the twenty-third floor.

FIFI   Ms. Muchly...

MUCHLY   There are laws that protect us, little miss. But there are no laws protecting our male counterparts.

FIFI   There are so.

MUCHLY   None that are implemented. If it's a woman's word against a man's, who do you think will be believed? Nobody's ever heard of a male victim.

FIFI   I suppose.

MUCHLY   I can say whatever I want to a man with no consequences. I can do things to him.

Inappropriate things that will make him quiver.

FIFI   How venomous.

MUCHLY   I can grab him, seduce him. Pull him into my bedchamber like a master puppeteer. I know his weak spots. I know how to get what I want.

FIFI   I didn't realize.

MUCHLY   They call us the weaker sex. *(laughs)* As long as we continue to let them believe that...

FIFI   I seem to have been going about this in the wrong way.

MUCHLY   If you have been victimized, it's only because you have allowed yourself to be. Remember who's in control.

FIFI   On the other hand...

MUCHLY   To hell with the other hand! This is no time to grow a conscience! Men are trying to take over the world and we musn't let them!

FIFI   But...

MUCHLY   They deserve it! Think of how they oppressed us throughout the days of yore!

FIFI   Of yore?

MUCHLY   Of frigging yore! Do something to save yourself! Stop whining and be a woman! *(composing herself)* Think about it.

ACT TWO, SCENE THREE

NIGEL's desk. NIGEL looks around to see if anyone is watching. When the coast is clear, he picks up his phone and dials. The phone rings on FIFI's desk.

NIGEL   *(on phone, disguising his voice)* Sorry you missed my call again, Ms. Sandcastle. Seems every time I call, you're away from your desk. This is Arthur Upton from Maygrover Enterprises. I'd like to discuss my account, if you please.

Enter FIFI, who discovers NIGEL on the phone. NIGEL is oblivious to her presence. He continues talking on the phone.

NIGEL   We at Maygrover Enterprises strive for excellence. We know you won't let us down, Ms. Sandcastle our hope is to utilize Ooford Inc. as a springboard for Maygrover's success. Don't bother returning my call. It's never necessary, as you may have figured out by now. I will phone later with further details on my vision for Maygr...

FIFI   You little weed.

NIGEL   Fifi.

GRUNT   I told you this would never work.

FIFI   What do you think you're doing, Nigel?

NIGEL   I have absolutely no idea what you're talking about.

FIFI   Don't lie!

NIGEL   You shouldn't be listening in on my personal calls.

                                 FIFI plays back her messages
                                 to reveal NIGEL's voice.

FIFI   Explain yourself.

NIGEL   Whatever you're accusing me of, you have no
               proof.

FIFI   Nigel...

NIGEL   That voice doesn't even sound like me. Boris will
               never believe...

FIFI   Nigel...

NIGEL   It was a harmless prank.

FIFI   My job is not some sort of a joke. You can't just go
               around tampering with my accounts. Sure, you do a
               great impersonation of Arthur Upton, but how am I
               supposed to know which messages are legit when
               you...

>*NIGEL and GRUNT stifle laughter.*

FIFI What's funny? What?

>*NIGEL and GRUNT stifle more laughter.*

FIFI Nigel, how many of these prank messages have you been leaving on my machine?

>*NIGEL and GRUNT stifle more laughter.*

FIFI I'm glad to see that my career is so amusing to the two of you. But I've no time for your adolescent games. Nigel, we are not in junior high school anymore. The Maygrover Account is real.

>*NIGEL and GRUNT burst out in laughter.*

FIFI The Maygrover Account is real.

NIGEL *(laughing)* Fifi, stop! You're killing me!

FIFI It is real, isn't it?

GRUNT How many times have you actually spoken to Arthur Upton in person?

FIFI Oh God. What are you saying?

NIGEL   Maygrover was the name of the poodle I had as a kid.

FIFI   Maygro...There is no...My account. My job...My...God no. God no. God no.

GRUNT   Get the lady a chair, Nigel. She's about to swoon.

FIFI   I am not about to...Nigel Inksplotch, How could you do this...Why would you...What reason could you possibly have...

NIGEL   For six months you've fallen for my clever plan.

FIFI   This account is the only thing keeping me from getting outsourced. How am I going to explain this to Mr. Putterson?

GRUNT   You're a competent uterus. I'm sure you'll brew up some words, seasoned with savvy.

FIFI   Nigel, if you care about me as much as you say you do, why would you...

GRUNT   Because he can.

FIFI   What?

NIGEL   Sooner or later you're going to have to come to terms with the fact that I know what's best for you. We were meant to be together, you and I.

FIFI   I can make my own decisions.

NIGEL	And what I have done has given you the freedom to believe such tripe.
FIFI	I worked hard...
NIGEL	Because of me.
FIFI	I had a job to do...
NIGEL	Because of me.
FIFI	I thought I was happy.
NIGEL	I have always been the one with the power to make you happy.
FIFI	Depraved. You are a sick, sick man and this demented power plot will no longer work.
NIGEL	It has worked since the sixth grade.
FIFI	What?
NIGEL	I have altered every decision you have made since you were twelve years old. You're just unaware of it. But you must believe me when I say that my motives were pure.
FIFI	Says the compulsive liar.
NIGEL	Fifi...
FIFI	My name is Clarissa.

NIGEL   I hardly think so.

FIFI   You have no power over me. Do you understand? I have the power.

GRUNT   Please.

FIFI   I have something you want, Nigel. Do you understand? I can make things happen for you or I can rub you out and blow you away like loose eraser shavings.

NIGEL   What the...

> FIFI *clears off her desk with one fell swoop of her arm.*

FIFI   I am not going to be a victim anymore. Want what I have? Do you?

NIGEL   Fifi...

FIFI   I'm aware of your weaknesses, Nigel. You've wanted this since the sixth grade. Do you want me to give it to you or not?

GRUNT   Holy frig.

NIGEL   Fifi, what are you doing?

FIFI   I am about to use you to get what I want. We are about to have pre-marital, unprotected, carnal, iniquitous, profane, gratuitous, unconsenting...stuff on this here desk. Grunt, come over here and tell the man how it's done.

NIGEL   Fifi...

FIFI   *(forcing NIGEL on desk, forcing his arms down)* And you can't call it rape because nobody's ever heard of a male victim.

NIGEL   *(being held down)* I'm okay with that.

FIFI   *(loosening grip)* And yet you repulse me.

NIGEL   So?

FIFI   I can't do this.

NIGEL   What? You were about to violate me! You can't change your mind now!

FIFI   Don't think my scruples make me frail. I can still leave you dangling.

NIGEL   Temptress! You can't make empty promises to do offensive things to my body! That's immoral!

                    Enter ROBIN, leading FONDA into the office on a leash.

FIFI   Robin.

NIGEL   Oh, this is just great. I suppose you're going to violate him instead because he has nicer hair.

ROBIN   Clarissa, I need some closure.

GRUNT   Closure? What are you? A girl?

NIGEL   This is not the end, Fifi. I am not going to allow this to end!

Exit NIGEL.

GRUNT   Stupid woman. You almost had him.

ACT TWO, SCENE FOUR

> *BORIS's office. He is on the phone, spinning on his swivel chair.*

BORIS   Numbers, Irv. What did I tell you about those numbers? I am responsible for the elephantine size of these digits. That's right, Irv. I am a numerical fool. *(pretentious laugh)* Yeah, I just made that one up.

> *Enter IDA, carrying a cardboard box.*

IDA   Mr. Putterson.

BORIS   *(on phone)* Sorry, Irv. Someone of little importance just arrived. I'll prudently deal with it and get back to you. *(hangs up)* You still here?

IDA   I packed my box.

BORIS   Away with you, then.

IDA   Any last words before I hit the bricks?

BORIS   You're taking on a rather negative tone.

IDA   You're not exactly my boss anymore.

BORIS   Your point being?

IDA	I make a habit of saving my respect for those who deserve it.
BORIS	I seldom waste time talking to unimportant people, but I'll explain something to you, nonetheless, because I'm such a swell guy. I have to get rid of all the unimportant specks who work beneath me. If I manage unimportant people, it will make me look unimportant and as we both know, my job is the most pivotal in the company.
IDA	I am not unimportant.
BORIS	You have illusions of grandeur.
IDA	I'm a secretary.
BORIS	Even so, there is a danger in trying to be something you're not. Grasping for something out of reach.
IDA	Really.
BORIS	People like you will always submit to people like me.
IDA	Like you.
BORIS	People in this office respect me. You know why?
IDA	Because you force them?
BORIS	Because I am the quintessential man.

IDA	Mr. Putterson...
BORIS	Power so spicy you can taste it. *(pretentious laugh)* Power has a flavour, you know.
IDA	Mr. Putterson...
BORIS	Power tastes sort of like pepper-jack cheese.
IDA	Mr. Putterson...
BORIS	I'm fond of power.
IDA	It's overrated.
BORIS	Come again?
IDA	Power. It's never been all that important to me.
BORIS	Which works out well because you have so little of it.
IDA	What good is power if everybody hates you?
BORIS	That certainly doesn't apply to me. *(pretentious laugh)*
IDA	It's not worth it.
BORIS	I'm not asking you.
IDA	The most empowering thing in the world is to be surrounded by people who care about you.

BORIS   I love me.

IDA   At least someone does.

BORIS   Oh, stop it, you little speck. Everyone in this building worships me. I mean, I have this swivel chair.

IDA   Everyone in this building mocks you. They burst into uncontrollable fits of laughter whenever you leave a room. You are the company joke.

BORIS   Important people like me do not have to listen to secretarial babble. I'm going to buzz my secretary and have you removed from the building.

IDA   You don't have a secretary.

BORIS   Every important man has a secretary.

IDA   And yet, you haven't one.

BORIS   You're making me need a coffee. I'll just buzz...

IDA   Who? Who are you going to buzz, Boris?

BORIS   Curses! Who is going to make me coffee?

IDA   You could make it yourself.

BORIS   But I'm important.

IDA   I suppose you'll have to hire another lowly

secretary, if you can degrade yourself to such a base deed.

BORIS   I'm on it. I'll just get my secretary to drum up some paperwork and...

IDA   Boris...

BORIS   Mary and Joseph! My life is unravelling like a cheap sweater!

IDA   Sorry to hear it. I'll be leaving now.

BORIS   Ida! Don't leave me!

IDA   Do I have something you want?

BORIS   Don't play that game with me. Important people need secretaries!

IDA   In that case, there's no need for me to be here. *(leaves)*

BORIS   Ida!

ACT TWO, SCENE FIVE

> *FIFI's office. FIFI and ROBIN are standing by FIFI's desk. FONDA, still wearing a leash around her neck, is seated alone at NIGEL's empty desk. GRUNT is staring at FONDA inappropriately.*

ROBIN   It's understandable that you would misread my intentions, my hair being as great as it is.

FIFI   If I was Hamlet, you would be my tragic flaw.

ROBIN   My hair often confuses women.

FIFI   Your hair.

ROBIN   I can't help it. Women find well-coiffed men fetching. I have absolutely no control over the effect my hair has on people.

> *FONDA begins sharpening pencils in the electric pencil sharpener.*

FIFI   Robin, you obviously don't understand what I'm feeling.

ROBIN   Excuse me. *(to FONDA)* Fonda, Love. Can you please stop doing that? It's most distracting.

FIFI   Robin, why are you so oblivious? Can you not see how you've...

ROBIN   Clarissa, whatever issues you need to work out have nothing to do with me. It's between you and my hair.

GRUNT   *(approaching FONDA)* Wanna' neck?

FONDA   No thank you. I already have one.

GRUNT   The name's John Grunt. And you are the most voluptuous thing I've ever seen.

FONDA   I'm Fonda Yoo.

GRUNT   I'm fonda' you too.

FONDA   I thought your name was John.

FIFI   Robin, I...I cared...

ROBIN   I know. My hair is a big deal. But we both know it's not enough to build a relationship on. I'm vain and insensitive and even I know that.

FONDA   *(to GRUNT)* You do not smell as good as Robin, but you are very friendly.

GRUNT   You don't know the half of it, Sweet Cheeks.

FONDA   You mean you can smell worse than you do now?

FIFI   You are not an easy man to get over.

ROBIN   I know, Love. I know.

FIFI   And look who I lost out to. Fonda.

ROBIN   Be nice to Fonda.

FIFI   She's a few fleas short of a St. Bernard.

ROBIN   Fonda has qualities. *(leaving)* Qualities you wouldn't understand.

                                GRUNT grabs FONDA's behind.

FONDA   *(startled)* Ooo!

GRUNT   Nice. Just like a squeezable plush toy.

FONDA   Are you objectifying me?

                                FIFI perks up.

GRUNT   *(grabbing FONDA's behind)* What is your problem?

FONDA   *(slapping GRUNT)* Mephistophelian imp!

FIFI   *(slowly)* Fonda, where did you learn that word?

FONDA   *(recovering herself)* I was confused in my head! I was confused in my head! I was confused in my head!

FIFI   You're supposed to be an imbecile. What's with the Oxfordian utterances?

FONDA   *(exhaling and converting to a composed persona)* Okay, look. I am not a cretin as one might suppose. I am a highly cerebral woman with an IQ higher than most national deficits. Most recently I completed my dissertation on gravity.

FIFI   Gravity?

FONDA   I disagree with it.

FIFI   That' impossible.

FONDA   One would think. However, I successfully argued my thesis, convincing the faculty, along with the top academics in my field and as a result, the Law of Gravity was vetoed and hence, no longer exists.

FIFI   What the...

FONDA   I think outside of the box.

FIFI   If you're so smart, why would you...

FONDA   It was the hair.

FIFI   Hair?

FONDA   Robin's hair sucked me in. I was weak, I admit. But it is common knowledge that men are intimidated by cerebral women, so I had to morph into a creature of intellect inferior to that of Robin. That was quite a task, I assure you.

FIFI   But...

FONDA   Don't get puritanical on me. You would do the same thing to win Robin's affection. I however, was successful.

FIFI   Successful?

FONDA   I don't see anything of the male persuasion on your arm.

FIFI   Fonda...

FONDA   Don't tell Robin.

FIFI   What?

FONDA   I'll lose everything. I may have an infinite scope of knowledge, but lonely is the life of an intelligent woman.

FIFI   Fonda...

FONDA   He has such great hair.

FIFI   Yes, but...

FONDA   It will all be worth it in the end because you know the kind of man I'll end up with!

> *GRUNT hits FONDA over the head with a club and carries her limp body over his shoulder. He takes her offstage.*

FIFI   Fonda!

ACT TWO, SCENE SIX

>*BORIS is restless at his desk. He fidgets. He looks around impatiently. His leg is involuntarily shaking and he twitches occasionally. The phone rings.*

BORIS *(answers phone quickly)* Numbers?...You have the wrong number. *(hangs up)*

>*BORIS fidgets some more, pushing papers on his desk.*

BORIS Important papers on my desk. Lots and lots of important papers. Important. Important. That's what I am. I don't need a secretary. Noooo sir. I'm above that. I have a swivel chair. An office with a window. A suit. Even my suit is important. And what about my numbers? Didn't I always tell you how significantly large my numbers are? My numbers? My...dwindling numbers? And what about my sickening levels of testosterone? Yup. Got so much man juice, makes me grow hair on my tongue. Got me five kids to prove it. Five kids. One, two, three, four, five kids. That oughta' tell you something...Although none of them are biologically mine. I inherited them from my drunk brother who was declared unfit. But that, in no way, affects my virile abilities.

>*Phone rings.*

BORIS   *(answering quickly)* How the heck are ya?...Irv? Do I have numbers? Do I have?...*(looks around nervously)* About the numbers, Irv. My numbers are sort of...small. I have to get out of this place, Irv. The walls are compressing around me like an accordion. The flickering, fluorescent lights are making fun of me. My swivel chair won't swivel, I'm not on speaking terms with my computer and I don't know how to make coffee. I recently heard a rumor that the CEO has plans to remove me from my office and replace me with a ping pong table. He thinks it will boost company morale. Morale, Irv! I'm against that! Do you suppose anyone suspects that I have absolutely no idea what I'm doing? Do you think they suspect that you're my hairdresser?...Forget about it, Irv. The stress is killing me! I'm going to buzz my secretary and have her book me some airline tickets to Punta Cana. My secretary. I have no secretary! *(slumps out to his chair and slinks lifelessly onto the floor)* Nuuuuuuumbers!

ACT TWO, SCENE SEVEN

> *FIFI is sitting alone at her desk.*

FIFI   Balance. Why won't these numbers balance? My life is a frigging typhoon! Why won't anything balance? I hate numbers! *(balls up paper and tosses it)* Is this normal? I want to be normal, please. I want to want normal things. I want to want kids. I want to not care so much about my career. I want a job and still be a woman. I want a man and still have self-respect. I want these stupid numbers to balance. What am I looking for? I'm looking so hard. So hard. I'm looking. Looking. Where? Where?

> *Enter NIGEL, followed by GUS the security guard. NIGEL has the entire top of his head bandaged.*

NIGEL   *(pointing at FIFI)* There she is! She's the one who did this to me!

FIFI   Nigel!

NIGEL   She is the guilty one! Take her away!

FIFI   Nigel, what happened to your head?

NIGEL   As if you didn't know!

GUS   Are you sure this is the woman who attacked you, Mr. Inksplotch?

NIGEL   The very one!

FIFI   Attacked you? Nigel, what are you talking about?

GUS   Calm down, Mr. Inksplotch. Tell me what happened.

NIGEL   I saw her do it. That's why she assaulted me!

FIFI   Saw me do what?

NIGEL   Shut up! *(to GUS)* Mr. Security Guard, Fifi is the one who stole the diamond necklace! I saw her do it when I was at the jewellers getting the battery replaced in my watch. When the clerk took my watch into the back, Fifi took a baseball bat and smashed the glass showcase. She snatched the necklace, laughed diabolically and was about to escape through the front door. There wasn't much time to think, so I apprehended her. Before I knew what was happening, she took out a nine iron and bludgeoned me repeatedly over the head! I'm not sure how long I was unconscious. I just remember waking up on the cold linoleum with one heck of a headache. There was no sign of Fifi or the necklace. Fifi had escaped!

FIFI   Gus, you have to believe me when I say that this all comes as quite a shock to me.

GUS   Mr. Inksplotch, how well do you know the suspect?

NIGEL   We're engaged.

GUS   But how well do you really know her?

NIGEL   The intern in the emergency room said I'm lucky to be alive. This woman is extremely dangerous. I suggest you put her in shackles and lock her up before she fractures some other poor wretch's skull.

FIFI   Gus, please. You don't honestly believe...

GUS   Mr. Inksplotch, would you say you respect the suspect?

NIGEL   Sixty-two stitches. And I think I might have some mild brain damage.

GUS   Do you even know her name?

FIFI   Gus, I can't believe you're taking his side!

NIGEL   Aha! She's wearing the stolen necklace right now! See? It's on her scrawny neck!

                                    FIFI feels her neck and gasps.

FIFI   But...But Nigel. You gave me this necklace.

NIGEL   She stammered! Did you hear that? She stammered! That's what liars do when they can't think of a response! I know these things!

GUS   What are your intentions, Mr. Inksplotch?

NIGEL   I want Fifi put in handcuffs.

GUS   That's what I thought.

NIGEL   Why have you not locked her up yet? Why has justice not been achieved?

FIFI   Gus...

NIGEL   It's because she's a lady, isn't it?

GUS   She is a lady.

NIGEL   You're going to take her word over mine because you don't think a lady is capable of doing something unrefined! She's not nibbling crumpets at a Gatsby garden party! She clocked me on the loaf with a nine iron!

FIFI   Go ahead, Gus. Do the wrong thing. I'm waiting.

NIGEL   I know what you're thinking. Nobody's ever heard of a male victim. Well, it's not true! I have been victimized at the hand of this shrew! She's not the frail one! I am! Me!

GUS   Mr. Inksplotch, have you even bothered asking for her side of the story?

NIGEL   Her side of the...How dare you discriminate against me for being a man! You're suspecting the worst of me because I don't wear a bra...often.

GUS   Mmmhmmm. That's what I thought. *(taking NIGEL's arm)* We need to have a little chat in the security office.

NIGEL   *(shaking off GUS's grasp)* Unhand me!

> *In an attempt to escape GUS's grasp, NIGEL struggles and several diamonds, which were hidden in his jacket, are scattered all over the floor.*

NIGEL   Fifi, look what you've done!

GUS   *(putting handcuffs on NIGEL)* Classy.

NIGEL   I'm innocent! Innocent, I tell ya! Fifi's the one you want! I'm just an unassuming victim!

GUS   He won't be bothering you anymore, Clarissa.

FIFI   I could have taken care of it myself, if I absolutely had to.

GUS   I know.

NIGEL   Interrogate me all you want! I'll just lie! I can screw with your head!

> *FIFI looks busy at her desk as GUS drags NIGEL offstage. As*

he is leaving, GUS steals a glance at FIFI, who does not notice him. GUS smiles shyly and leaves.

ACT TWO, SCENE EIGHT

FIFI is left alone at her desk. She is seated and working. ROBIN, GRUNT, NIGEL, BORIS, IDA, FONDA and MS. MUCHLY randomly appear in various spots on the stage. Each is spotlit and isolated. It is as though their lines are occurring inside FIFI's head.

ROBIN   My hair.

GRUNT   Wanna' neck?

NIGEL   You're mine.

BORIS   Unimportant.

IDA   I'm so happy.

FONDA   *(stupidly)* I'm Fonda Yoo.

MUCHLY   Power.

ROBIN   It's all about my hair.

GRUNT   Sizzling butt cheeks.

NIGEL   Mine.

BORIS   Numbers.

IDA   I had a job once.

FONDA   Brains? What for?

MUCHLY   Make things happen.

BORIS   There's no place for you here.

IDA   Have a baby.

NIGEL   You don't have a choice.

ROBIN   I don't want to get out of your head.

GRUNT   Don't make me force you.

IDA   Look how happy I am!

BORIS   At least I have my numbers.

FONDA   Men are...

ROBIN   Hot.

GRUNT   On fire.

NIGEL   In control.

BORIS   Important.

MUCHLY	Pathetic.

IDA   Perfect in every way.

FONDA   I'm confused in my head!

> *Fade out ROBIN, GRUNT, NIGEL, BORIS, IDA, FONDA and MS. MUCHLY.*

FIFI   *(at her desk)* Confused in my head! *(looking at her watch)* Why am I still here? Why am I still working late when I know there's no job for me? I've got to stop being such a woman. Stop internalizing every blasted thing. Why try to figure out my job, my life, men. Why try to rationalize the illogical? Forget about Robin. Forget about these masculine grasshoppers who plague my life. I'm destined to be alone, so why stew over it? That Ida. I bet there is no Samuel. She probably made him up. There is no man who's perfect for me. How can there be? Look what I have to pick from?

> *Enter GUS.*

GUS   Clarissa?

FIFI   I didn't call for you.

GUS   It's late and your car is still in the parking lot.

FIFI   If I needed you I would have called for you.

GUS   It's dark outside. I just thought...

FIFI   I am perfectly capable of walking to my own car.

GUS   I read in the paper there's a sex pervert on the loose.

FIFI   Only one?

GUS   Is everything okay?

FIFI   I have decided to have a very bad attitude about men.

GUS   ...Oh.

FIFI   I don't trust them. Not a one. There's a lot of sick bastards out there who would jump at the chance to hurt me. Attack me. Break me. Control me. Why, might you ask? Because they can!

GUS   But for every jerk out there who wants to hurt you, there's ten nice guys who would step in and defend you.

FIFI   Are you deaf? I don't want to be defended! I can take care of myself!

GUS   But...

FIFI   You are so naïve. You don't know the first thing about men.

GUS	I guess not.
FIFI	Was that sarcasm? Are you patronizing me?
GUS	No.
FIFI	You're a liar. You're no different from the rest of them.
GUS	Clarissa...
FIFI	My name is Fifi!
GUS	No it isn't.
FIFI	Stop making sense. It confuses me.
GUS	Clarissa, not all men are...
FIFI	Yes they are! All men are base creatures. I can't find one gentleman in this sea of barnacles and believe me, I've looked.
GUS	Not in the right places.
FIFI	*(leaving)* I am going to walk to my car. Alone. I don't need a man to hold my hand in the dark. Especially not you.
GUS	But...
FIFI	I don't need you, Gus!

Exit FIFI. Dejected, GUS sighs and pulls a bouquet of daisies out of his jacket. He examines them disappointedly, then tosses them in the waste can. Exit GUS. A moment later, FIFI rushes back in.

FIFI   Stupid car keys. I always leave them on my...

FIFI notices something in the waste can. She takes the flowers out and looks at them, confused. She then looks at the door through which GUS left.

Finis.

www.ingramcontent.com/pod-product-compliance
Lightning Source LLC
Chambersburg PA
CBHW052011170626

46808CB00007B/2872